LEGO® KNIGHTS' KINGDOM

Search for the King

by Daniel Lipkowitz

Illustrated by Mada Design, Inc.

SCHOLASTIC INC.

New York   Toronto   London   Auckland   Sydney

Mexico City   New Delhi   Hong Kong   Buenos Aires

No part of this publication may be reproduced in whole or in part, stored in a retrieval system, or transmitted in any form or by any means, electronic, mechanical, photocopying, recording, or otherwise, without written permission of the publisher. For information regarding permission, write to Scholastic Inc., Attention: Permissions Department, 557 Broadway, New York, NY 10012.

ISBN 0-439-70230-5

© 2005 The LEGO Group. LEGO, the LEGO logo, KNIGHTS' KINGDOM, and the KNIGHTS' KINGDOM logo are registered trademarks of The LEGO Group and are used here by special permission. All rights reserved. Published by Scholastic Inc.
SCHOLASTIC and associated logos are trademarks and/or registered trademarks of Scholastic Inc.

12 11 10 9 8 7 6 5 4 3   5 6 7 8 9/0

Designed by Rick DeMonico

Printed in the U.S.A.
First printing, April 2005

Chapter 1
A Team of Heroes

BOOM! The arena shook with the force of the blow. A red knight charged at a dragon. *CRASH!* The wooden beast exploded in a shower of splinters.

"Well done, Santis!" called out a knight in purple armor. "But don't just rely on your strength. Sometimes you need to think your way past danger."

"I'll leave the thinking to you, Danju," said a knight in green as he somersaulted through a ring high above the ground. He spun and balanced with an acrobat's skill. "Rascus is all about action!"

Danju leaned on his wolf-symbol shield and smiled. There was something about Rascus that made people smile. "Just remember to keep your feet on the ground once in a while, my friend," he said.

Danju looked around the training field. "Where has Jayko run off to now?" he asked.

"Here I am, Danju!" Jayko called. He was training with a knight-shaped target. *Swing, block, dodge, strike!* The young knight's arm blurred as his sword moved faster and faster. "Now watch these moves!" he cried.

Santis was brushing splinters off his bear-symbol shield. He paused to watch. "Jayko has something special," he said in his deep, rumbling voice.

Danju nodded. "His speed is amazing," he said. "But he still has a lot to learn. See?"

Jayko had been so busy showing off his swordsmanship that he had forgotten to watch where he was going. He tripped over the pieces of the smashed wooden dragon and went flying . . . right into the pole beneath Rascus' ring!

"Whoa!" the green knight cried out as the ring started to topple. He flipped in the air like the monkey on his shield, then began to fall. Rascus would have landed right on his head if Santis hadn't caught him.

"My thanks to you, Santis," Rascus said. "That was a little too much action, even for me!"

Jayko lay on the ground in a heap. "Ow," he said. "What hit me?"

Danju stood over him. "Jayko the Quick you may be," he said, "but maybe not Jayko the Quick-thinking." The older knight smiled kindly as he held out a hand. "You need to learn to look before you leap, youngster. You'll never win the tournament at this rate."

Jayko got to his feet. He picked up his hawk-symbol shield and golden sword. "I've got to do my best," he said. "One day, I'm going to be a great hero."

Chapter 2
A Sinister Scheme

A knight in black armor kneeled before the throne. "Your Majesty," he said, "you have ruled Morcia for a long time."

King Mathias stroked his gray beard. "That is true," he said. "The years have caught up with me." But the king was contented. "Yet they have been good years," he said. "My kingdom is at peace, and the Book of Morcia tells me that the people are happy." He pointed toward a large book that lay open on a stand nearby.

The magical pages of the Book of Morcia contained all the wisdom and knowledge in the kingdom. It was the king's most prized and useful possession.

"All thanks to your wise rule," said the knight. His name was Vladek and he was the king's advisor. "The Knights of Morcia have not gone to battle in many years. The creatures of the Desolate Moorlands no longer invade your kingdom. We hardly have a need for knights at all."

King Mathias considered his advisor's words. "But my knights are loyal and brave," he said. "And the people love watching them in the tournaments."

Vladek smiled craftily. The conversation was going just as he had planned.

"Then perhaps it is time for a new tournament, Your Majesty," he said. "One finer and greater than any before. Let us announce a Grand Tournament."

A Grand Tournament was a very special event. It was held when a king retired. The winner of a Grand

Tournament became the new king!

"A Grand Tournament . . ." The king considered the idea. He did sometimes wish to live the life of a simple knight again, as he had before the last Grand Tournament many years ago.

King Mathias had known Vladek for as long as he had been king. He usually trusted Vladek's advice, but he sometimes suspected that the knight wanted to be king himself.

King Mathias shook his head. "Thank you for your advice, Vladek," he said, "but my heart tells me to stay. I will remain king at least a while longer."

Vladek had been sure that the king would call for a new Grand Tournament — one that Vladek himself would win using dark magic he had studied. He rose angrily and snapped his fingers. Several knights stepped into the room. They wore Vladek's scorpion symbol on their black armor, and their eyes were red and strange.

"Morcia *will* have a new king," Vladek said as his

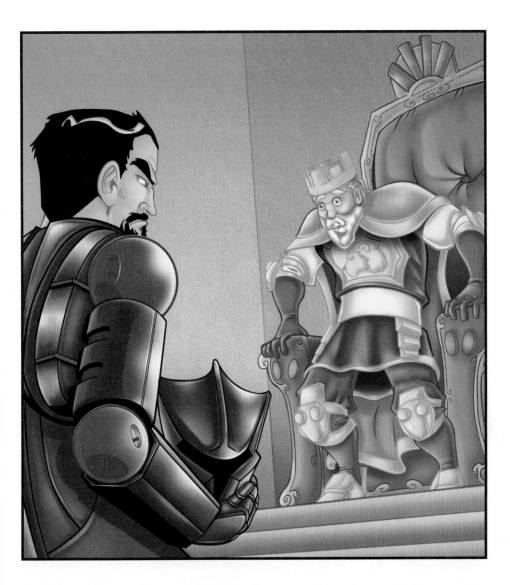

knights moved toward the throne. "And it will be me!"

The next morning, word spread across Morcia: The king had vanished!

Chapter 3
A Grand Proclamation

The knights searched everywhere, but they could not find the king.

When enough time had passed, Vladek called the people together.

"People of Morcia," Vladek said, "we have found no trace of King Mathias. Even the Book of Morcia can tell us nothing about his whereabouts. As his royal advisor, I have had to rule the kingdom in his absence. But Morcia needs a real king. If Mathias does not return soon, we must hold a new Grand Tournament!"

A whisper ran through the crowd.

"The knight who wins the lightning duels of the Grand Tournament will become the new king," Vladek said. He smiled wickedly. "Of course, I myself shall enter." Vladek drew his sword and held it high up in the air. "May the most noble knight win!"

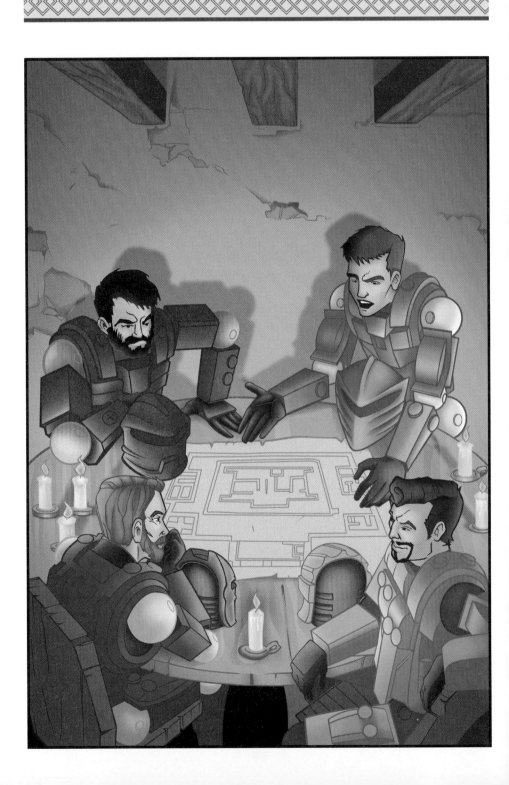

Chapter 4
A Secret Meeting

Four knights sat at a table. They were not happy.

Jayko was the first to speak. "Vladek is cruel and unjust, and anyone who disagrees with him is thrown into prison," he said.

"Vladek has his own knights now," Santis said. "He calls them Shadow Knights, and they obey only him. No one knows who they are or where they came from."

"It's worse than that," said Rascus. "There are fewer Knights of Morcia every day. It's as if every knight loyal to the king is disappearing, one by one."

Danju spoke last. "I do not trust Vladek," he said, "and I do not believe that King Mathias has simply vanished." The wise knight looked around the table. "I think that Vladek and his Shadow Knights have captured the king and locked him away."

"But where could he be?" asked Jayko. "We've

looked everywhere!" Rascus and Santis nodded.

"Not everywhere. There is one place where we have not searched," Danju said. He pointed to a map of the great Castle of Morcia. "We have not looked in the king's castle. We will go there tonight!"

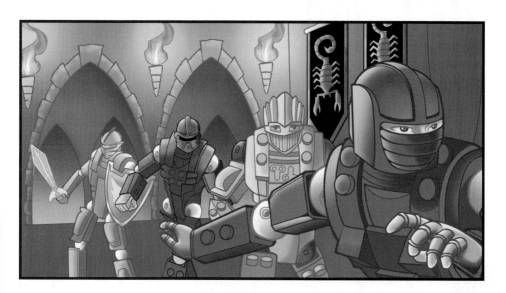

Chapter 5
A Slight Miscalculation

In the dark of night, the knights crept up to the castle gates. They slipped past the guards and made their way inside. Flickering torches and scorpion banners were everywhere.

"I don't like what Vladek's done with the place," Rascus whispered to the others.

Danju led the way. He pointed toward a flight of steep stone stairs. "The castle dungeon must be down there," he said. "If Vladek is keeping the king a prisoner, that is where we will find him."

Rascus looked at the stairs. "I think I hear more Shadow Knights," he said.

"Then we should be careful," Santis said in a low rumble. "And *quiet*." He looked at Rascus, who was not known for being silent. But Rascus nodded. He knew how serious this mission was.

Jayko drew his sword. "I'm the quickest, so I'll run ahead and try to find the king!" he said.

"Jayko, wait!" Danju whispered. "We need a plan!"

But Jayko was already halfway down the stairs and moving faster with every step.

Suddenly, there was a loud click. With a terrible grinding, a heavy stone wall slid down at the top of the staircase. The three knights were trapped on the other side!

"Jayko's all alone down there!" Rascus said.

"That young knight is going to get himself in trouble

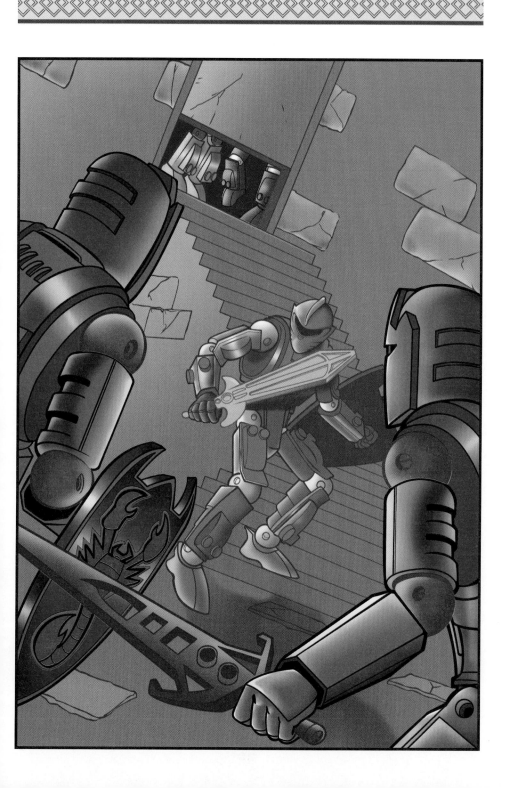

one day," Danju sighed.

In fact, Jayko was already in trouble. As he reached the bottom of the stairs, he found himself face-to-face with a pair of surprised Shadow Knights.

The Shadow Knights stared at Jayko with their strange red eyes. "Halt!" one commanded.

Jayko wasn't worried. Two Shadow Knights wouldn't be a problem for a knight of his speed and skill! He pointed his sword at them. "Tell me where the king is!" he said.

Five more Shadow Knights stepped around the corner. "We serve no king but Vladek!" one said as the others drew their swords.

Uh-oh, thought Jayko, realizing that he had just made a big mistake. But a Knight of Morcia never surrenders. He raised his hawk shield as the Shadow Knights marched toward him.

Chapter 6
A Daring Rescue

CRASH!

A huge crack appeared in the stone wall at the top of the stairs. There was another crash, and the wall fell down in a pile of rubble!

Standing on the other side was Santis.

"Seven against one doesn't seem very fair," the Knight of the Bear said. "Need a hand, Jayko?"

The Knight of the Hawk grinned. "Nothing I can't handle," he said, "but feel free to join in!"

Danju, Rascus, and Santis ran down the stairs. "So much for the *quiet* plan," Rascus said as he jumped over the smashed stones.

"More Shadow Knights will be coming," Danju said. "We need to act quickly."

Jayko used his speed to disarm two of the Shadow Knights before they could even react. Rascus kept another pair busy with a series of wild leaps and flips. While the dark knights were distracted by the Knight of the Monkey's antics, Santis picked up one in each hand

and shook them until they dropped their swords.

The remaining three Shadow Knights surrounded Danju. "This old knight will be easy," one said.

"With age comes experience," Danju replied. His ancient blade wove skillfully through the air, and the Shadow Knights' swords clattered onto the floor. Surrounded and weaponless, the evil knights raised their hands and surrendered.

While Rascus tied up the captured knights, Santis rebuilt the broken wall. "This should keep out any more Shadow Knights," he said as he piled the last of the rocks at the top of the stairs.

Danju was looking around. "Strange," he said. "I'm sure that the dungeon is down here, but there are no doors out of this room."

"Maybe there's a secret passage?" Jayko suggested.

Danju nodded. "Perhaps," he said. "If so, we must find it quickly. Those rocks won't hold forever."

"No one escapes from Vladek!" one of the

captured Shadow Knights shouted. "He will chase you to the ends of the earth and punish you!"

"The only one who will be punished is Vladek," Danju said. "Now tell us where King Mathias is!"

"Never!" the dark knight said.

Santis wanted to break down more walls until they found the dungeon, but Danju thought that the ceiling might cave in. The Knight of the Wolf examined the room carefully. He tapped on the walls to see if any of them were hollow. He lifted the scorpion banners to look for hidden doors. He moved the torches in case one was a secret lever. But he couldn't find anything.

The Shadow Knights laughed. "You'll never find it!" one said. "Vladek is much too clever for you."

Danju watched the Shadow Knights carefully. "Actually," he said, "I have already discovered the secret door."

"You lie!" said one of the dark knights. He quickly looked at the stone staircase.

Danju smiled. "I did fib a little," he admitted. "But thanks to you, now I know that the dungeon is hidden beneath the stairs."

The Shadow Knight was silent, but the angry look on his face told the knights that Danju had guessed correctly.

The staircase looked as if it were made of solid stones, until Danju poked one of the rocks with the tip of his sword. There was a click and the sound of moving gears. The staircase slowly split in two, revealing a secret passage beneath. They had found the dungeon!

Chapter 7
A King's Mission

"My knights . . . at last you have come."

King Mathias sat on the floor of the dark prison cell. His royal robes were dirty and torn.

"Your Majesty!" Danju said.

Danju and Santis helped the king to stand. While Rascus looked out for guards, the knights and the king slipped through the castle corridors and outside.

In the safety of the forest, King Mathias spoke to the four knights.

"Thank you," he told them. "If not for you, I might have been Vladek's prisoner forever."

"Vladek has called for a Grand Tournament," Jayko said. "But now there is no need for a new king!"

King Mathias shook his head sadly. "Vladek has learned forbidden magic, and he has the Book of Morcia," he told the knights. "If I return, he will simply lock me up again . . . or worse."

The king told them how Vladek had used his magic to transform many of the Knights of Morcia into Shadow Knights. Only when the evil spell was broken would they be restored to their true selves.

"We must defeat him in the Grand Tournament!"

said Santis.

"Vladek's magic protects him in battle," King Mathias said. "He is too powerful for any knight to defeat on his own."

"Then what can we do?" Rascus asked.

"There is one thing," the king said. "Deep in the Desolate Moorlands stands an ancient tower. It is called the Citadel of Orlan."

"Orlan!" Jayko whispered. Every knight knew of the legendary First Knight, Orlan. Ages ago, he had defeated an evil sorcerer and saved Morcia. But his magic shield, the Shield of Ages, had been broken in the battle. No one knew where the fragments were hidden.

"One piece of the Shield of Ages remains," King Mathias said, "the stone at its center. It is called the Heart of the Shield, and it is locked away in the Citadel. Only the Heart has the power to protect a knight against Vladek's magic."

The king raised his hand in warning. "But the path

to the Citadel is not easy. Terrible creatures dwell in the Moorlands, and the tower is protected by great challenges. Only the most courageous have any hope of reaching the top."

The knights looked at one another. The fate of the entire kingdom rested with them.

Jayko spoke first. "We will find the Citadel of Orlan, Your Majesty," he said. "We will pass the challenges, and we will find the Heart of the Shield. We will return to defeat Vladek, and we will win the throne for the true king!"

King Mathias smiled. "Thank you, my good knights," he said. "I can see that you are brave. Trust in your skills and your friendship, and I know that you can succeed."

The four knights prepared for their long journey. This was the most important quest of their lives, but their adventure had just begun!

Up to a $60 Value!

Built For Fun!

LEGOLAND® California is built for real family fun, with more than 50 rides, shows and attractions. Everybody's sure to have a great time together, whether they're taking on hilarious challenges in the **Fun Town Fire Academy** fire truck race, experiencing the excitement of **Coasterauraus** and digging for fossils at **Dino Island**—or getting into the splash of things at **AQUAZONE® Wave Racers.** The fun is as close as Carlsbad, 30 minutes north of San Diego and one hour south of Anaheim. For Park information visit www. LEGOLAND.com.

Save $10
on one-day admission to LEGOLAND® California

Coupon entitles bearer to $10 off up to six full price one-day admissions. Valid only on the day of purchase at LEGOLAND. Not valid with any other discounts or offers. Children 2 and under are admitted free. Original coupon must be exchanged at the ticket booth at the time of ticket purchase. Restrictions apply Prices and hours subject to change without notice. **Not for resale. Expires March 31, 2007** Scholastic   A-1324   C/S-2324

LEGO

LEGOLAND
CALIFORNIA